U0099233

For Gemk,

Whose endless supply of ideas and honest critique made this possible.

感謝 Gemk

源源不絕的靈感及誠懇的建議讓這一切成真。

The Yawning Yeti
雪人打呵欠

Coleen Reddy　著

朱成梁　繪

薛慧儀　譯

三民書局

Tasha lived with her family in a small town.

It was hot in summer and cold in winter.

Tasha's favorite season was winter because she loved to ice skate.

塔莎和家人住在一個小小的城鎮裡。

這裡夏天很熱，冬天很冷。

塔莎最喜歡的季節是冬天，因為她最愛溜冰了。

3

4

One winter, it got very cold.
"I don't understand," thought Tasha.
"Yesterday it was 15°C; today, it is −15°C."
It was so cold that she couldn't even ice skate.

有一年冬天，天氣好冷好冷。
「我真搞不懂。」塔莎想，
「明明昨天還有15度，今天卻只有負15度而已。」
天氣凍得她都不能去溜冰了！

"Why is it so cold?" Tasha asked her mother.

"There is a yeti that lives in the mountains. Whenever he yawns it gets colder. But it's never been so cold before," said Tasha's mother.

6

「為什麼天氣這麼冷呢？」塔莎問媽媽。
「因為山裡住著一個雪人，只要他一打呵欠，天氣就會變得冷一點。
但是以前從來不會這麼冷呀！」塔莎的媽媽說。

7

"That's right," said Tom, Tasha's father. "I think we should visit the yeti and tell him that he is yawning too much."

8

「這就對了！」塔莎的爸爸湯姆說：「我想我們該去看看雪人，告訴他，他打呵欠打得太兇囉！」

9

The next day, Tasha went with her father up into the mountains.
Tasha felt really cold even though she was wearing
her favorite, warm yellow jacket.
At last, they reached a cave.

第二天，塔莎就和爸爸一塊兒到山裡去了。
即使穿著她最愛的黃色保暖夾克，塔莎還是覺得很冷。
終於，他們來到一座洞穴前面。

Tasha could hear someone yawning loudly.
"That must be the yawning yeti,"
thought Tasha.
Tasha and her father stood outside the cave,
hesitant to go in. Then Tasha spotted a yak
sitting outside the cave.

塔莎在洞口就聽到了好大的呵欠聲。
「那一定就是打呵欠的雪人了。」塔莎想。
塔莎和爸爸站在洞口外，猶豫著不知道該不該進去。
這時，塔莎瞧見有隻犛牛坐在洞口外。

The yak spoke to them, "I know why you're here.
I was expecting somebody. It's getting too cold, isn't it?"
Tasha and her dad didn't know what to do.
They were expecting a yeti but instead they found a yak.

這隻麝牛開口說話了：「我知道你們為什麼來到這裡，
我就知道會有人來。天氣變得太冷了，對不對？」
塔莎和爸爸感到不知所措。
他們原來想找的是雪人，卻碰上一隻麝牛。

Tom spoke up, "We're here about the weather...."
"Yes, yes, I know," interrupted the yak. "It's getting too cold
so you came here to speak to the yeti and
ask him to stop yawning so much."
Tasha and Tom nodded their heads
and Tasha was about to speak
when the yak spoke again.

16

湯姆開口了：「我們來這裡是因為天氣實在⋯⋯」
「是的，是的，我知道，」聾牛打斷他的話。「天氣實在太冷了，
所以你們來這裡想要和雪人談談，要他別打這麼多呵欠。」
塔莎和爸爸點點頭，當塔莎想要開口說話時，聾牛又開口了。

"Well, you can't do anything. That yeti yawns when he's bored
and right now he's really bored," continued the yak.
"Why...." Tasha tried to talk but again the yak interrupted her.

「唉！你們來也沒用。雪人無聊時就會打呵欠，
而現在他可真的是無聊透了呢！」犛牛繼續說。
「為什麼……」塔莎試著想說話，但犛牛又打斷了她。

"I'm the only friend he has. We normally talk, well,
I normally talk and sometimes we play card games.
Because of me, he doesn't get bored. But we're not friends anymore."

「我是他唯一的朋友。通常我們會聊聊天,嗯,其實多半都是我在講話,
有時候我們也會玩玩牌。就是因為有我,他才不會覺得無聊,
但現在我們已經不再是朋友了。」

21

"We were playing card games and then I said he was cheating
and then he called me a bore who couldn't shut up.
Now, I know I talk a lot but that yeti went too far.
All the same, I forgave him but he won't forgive me.
He won't even talk to me," said the yak.
Tasha decided to try talking to the yeti.

「我們本來在玩牌，
我說他作弊，他反罵我是個
喋喋不休的討厭鬼。好吧！我知道我話多，
但那個雪人這次也實在太過分了！
雖然我像往常一樣原諒了他，這次他卻
不肯原諒我，他甚至連話都不跟我說了。」
塔莎決定要試著和雪人談一談。

She walked in quietly. She could hear the yeti yawning.

By the time she got near him, her hair had frozen into a huge icicle.

她安靜地走進洞穴裡，清楚地聽到了雪人打呵欠的聲音。
等到她來到雪人面前，頭髮都已經凍成了一根好大的冰柱。

25

"What do you want?" roared the yeti.
Tasha began, "I'm from the village and
it's getting extremely cold. I can't even
leave my home because of the cold. It seems that you're
very bored and that's why you're yawning so much."

「你想幹什麼?」雪人大叫著。

塔莎開口說:「我是從村裡來的,今年天氣實在變得太冷了,
冷得我甚至都出不了門了。看來你好像很無聊的樣子,
所以才會打這麼多呵欠。」

"I can't help that. I'm not so young anymore," growled the yeti.

"I know," said Tasha. "But I met your friend, the yak, and he said...."

「沒辦法，我不再年輕了。」雪人吼了回去。
「我知道呀！」塔莎說，
　「但是我遇見你的朋友犛牛，他說……」

"I don't care about what that stupid yak said. Did he tell you that he made fun of my yodeling? I used to yodel and I was good at it. Sure, it caused a few avalanches but it was still good. And, he called me a fat, old snowman."

"But you are a fat, old snowman," Tasha quietly said.

「我才不管那隻笨聲牛說什麼呢！他有沒有告訴妳他取笑我唱山歌的事情啊？我以前常常唱山歌，而且唱得還不賴呢！當然啦，有時候會引起一些雪崩，但我唱的山歌還是很好聽的。而且，他還罵我是個又胖又老的雪人。」

「可是，你本來就是個胖胖的老雪人呀！」塔莎小聲地說。

But instead of getting angry,
the yeti started laughing.
"I suppose I am an old, fat snowman,"
chuckled the yeti.

雪人不但沒有生氣，反而還笑了起來。

「我想，我的確是個胖胖的老雪人。」雪人咯咯地笑著說。

"Okay, tell the yak I am willing to be his friend
if he never makes fun of my yodeling," said the yeti.

「好吧！告訴犛牛，如果他不再取笑我唱山歌，
我就願意繼續和他做朋友。」雪人說。

Tasha told the yak what the yeti said.
The yak went into the cave and Tasha and her dad
could hear lots of laughter a few minutes later.

塔莎把雪人說的話告訴麋牛。
於是麋牛走進洞穴裡，幾分鐘後，
塔莎和爸爸便聽到一陣陣開懷的笑聲傳出來。

A few days later, the weather was back to normal.
Tasha was ice-skating on the lake when she heard a noise.

幾天後，天氣開始恢復正常了。
有天塔莎在湖上溜冰的時候，聽見一陣噪音。

She looked up and saw an avalanche on the mountain.
"I suppose that the yeti has started yodeling again,"
thought Tasha to herself.

她抬頭一看，原來是山上發生了雪崩呢。
「我猜，雪人又在唱山歌了吧！」塔莎這麼想著。

雪人吊飾

工具與材料

1. 銀色亮片
2. 西卡紙
3. 剪刀或刀片
4. 膠水
5. 膠帶
6. 打洞機
7. 白色的線
8. 一個衣架

＊在做勞作之前，要記得在桌上先鋪一張紙或墊板，才不會把桌面弄得髒兮兮喔！

步驟

1. 在西卡紙上畫雪人的形狀（或其他不同的形狀，如聖誕樹、雪花、雪天使、鹿等等）來作吊飾。
2. 將畫好的形狀剪下來。
3. 用打洞機在圖形的上方打洞，或直接用刀片割出小洞。
4. 在圖形上塗膠水，然後灑上亮片。

5. 等膠水完全乾後，將白線的一端綁在吊飾上，另一端綁在衣架上（有的綁高，有的綁低）。
6. 最後用膠帶固定綁在衣架上的一端，這樣吊飾就不會滑來滑去囉！

你可以將吊飾掛在陽光照得到的地方，你的小雪人就會閃閃發亮喔！！

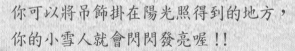

生字表

 *p. 6*

yeti [ˋjɛtɪ] 名 雪人
yawn [jɔn] 動 打呵欠

 p. 11

cave [kev] 名 洞穴

p. 12

hesitant [ˋhɛzətənt] 形 猶豫不決
的
spot [spɑt] 動 發現
yak [jæk] 名 犛牛

 *p. 14*

instead [ɪnˋstɛd] 副 代替；更換

 p. 20

normally [ˋnɔrməlɪ] 副 通常

 p. 22

bore [bor] 名 令人討厭的人
go too far 太過分

p. 24

freeze [friz] 動 使凍結
icicle [ˋaɪsɪkl̩] 名 冰柱

 p. 26

roar [ror] 動 怒吼，咆哮
extremely [ɪkˋstrimlɪ] 副 極度地

 p. 28

growl [graʊl] 動 吼叫

43

 *p. 30*

make fun of 嘲笑
yodel [`jodl̩] 動 唱山歌
avalanche [`ævə‚læntʃ] 名 雪崩；
　　山崩

 *p. 32*

instead of 取而代之的
suppose [sə`poz] 動 想，認為
chuckle [`tʃʌkl̩] 動 咯咯輕笑

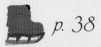 *p. 38*

normal [`nɔrml̩] 形 正常的

全新創作 英文讀本
帶給你優格（yogurt）般．青春的酸甜滋味！

Teens' Chronicles

愛閱雙語叢書

青春記事簿

大維的驚奇派對／秀寶貝，說故事／杰生的大秘密
傑克的戀愛初體驗／誰是他爸爸？
叛逆大維打工記／外星老師來上課／耶！放假了！

你我身上純真的影子，
透過一篇篇幽默風趣的故事重現，
推薦你這套青春無悔的創作系列，
讓愛玫、杰生、大維、凱爾、海倫、傑克，
帶你進入他們的世界，品味另一種學習英語的全新感受。

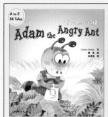

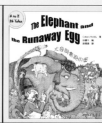

A to Z
26 Tales

二十六個妙朋友，陪你一起

愛閱雙語叢書

✿26個妙朋友系列✿

二十六個英文字母，二十六冊有趣的讀本，最適合初學英文的你！

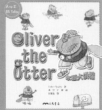

樂學英文！

精心錄製的雙語CD，
　　讓孩子學會正確的英文發音
用心構思的故事情節，
　　讓兒童熟悉生活中常見的單字
特別設計的親子活動，
　　讓家長和小朋友一起動動手、動動腦

國家圖書館出版品預行編目資料

The Yawning Yeti：雪人打呵欠 / Coleen Reddy著;
朱成梁繪; 薛慧儀譯. －－初版一刷. －－臺北
市; 三民, 2003
　　面; 　公分－－(愛閱雙語叢書. 二十六個妙朋
　　友系列) 中英對照
　　ISBN 957-14-3754-9 　(精裝)

　1.英國語言－讀本

523.38　　　　　　　　　　　　　92008794

© 　**The Yawning Yeti**
　　　　──雪人打呵欠

著作人　Coleen Reddy
繪　圖　朱成梁
譯　者　薛慧儀
發行人　劉振強
著作財
產權人　三民書局股份有限公司
　　　　臺北市復興北路386號
發行所　三民書局股份有限公司
　　　　地址／臺北市復興北路386號
　　　　電話／(02)25006600
　　　　郵撥／0009998-5
印刷所　三民書局股份有限公司
門市部　復北店／臺北市復興北路386號
　　　　重南店／臺北市重慶南路一段61號
初版一刷　2003年7月
編　號　S 85658-1
定　價　新臺幣壹佰捌拾元整
　行政院新聞局登記證局版臺業字第○二○○號

ISBN　957-14-3754-9　　(精裝)